W9-BAG-946

A Beginning-to-Read Book

Let's Go, Dear Dragon

by Margaret Hillert

Illustrated by Carl Kock

NORWOOD HOUSE PRESS

DEAR CAREGIVER,

The *Beginning-to-Read* series is a carefully written collection of classic readers you may remember from your own childhood. Each book features text comprised of common sight words to provide your child ample practice reading the words that appear most frequently in written text. The many additional details in the pictures enhance the story and offer the opportunity for you to help your child expand oral language and develop comprehension.

Begin by reading the story to your child, followed by letting him or her read familiar words and soon your child will be able to read the story independently. At each step of the way, be sure to praise your reader's efforts to build his or her confidence as an independent reader. Discuss the pictures and encourage your child to make connections between the story and his or her own life. At the end of the story, you will find reading activities and a word list that will help your child practice and strengthen beginning reading skills.

Above all, the most important part of the reading experience is to have fun and enjoy it!

Shannon Cannon

Shannon Cannon,
Literacy Consultant

Norwood House Press • P.O. Box 316598 • Chicago, Illinois 60631
For more information about Norwood House Press please visit our website at
www.norwoodhousepress.com or call 866-565-2900.

LIBRARY OF CONGRESS CATALOGING-IN-PUBLICATION DATA

    Let's go, dear dragon / by Margaret Hillert ; illustrated by Carl Kock.—
Rev. and expanded library ed.
      p. cm. — (Beginning to read series. Dear dragon)
    Summary: A boy and his pet dragon celebrate the Fourth of July by going to the beach, having a picnic, and watching fireworks. Includes reading activities.
  ISBN-13: 978-1-59953-021-5 (library edition : alk. paper)
  ISBN-10: 1-59953-021-X (library edition : alk. paper)
  1. Readers (Primary) [1. Readers.] I. Kock, Carl, ill. II. Title. III. Series.
PE1119.H57878 2006
  428.6–dc22   200503394

Get up. Get up.
This is a big day.
A big day for us.

Here.
Help me with this.
Make it go up.
Up, up, up.

And now come here.
Here is one for you.
You can have this one.

See what Mother and Father can do.
Mother and Father can make something.
Something good.
And we can help.

We work here too.
Father and I work.
The car looks good.

Get in the car now.
Get in with me.
We will ride, ride, ride.
We will have fun.

Away we go.
Away, away, away.
What a good day.

Here we are.
Get out. Get out.
We can play here.

Look what I can do to you.
No one can see you now.
No one can guess where you are.

See this.
I can make it go.
It can go up and up.
Get it. Get it.

Oh, my.
Look what you can do.
You are good at this.

We can do this, too.
Work, work, work.
We can do it.

Oh, oh, oh.
Help, help.
Look at us now.
You are too good.

Come with me now.
Come in here.
You will like it.

21

This looks good.
I want this
and this
and this.

You are a big help.
A big, big help.
Now you have one, too.
It is good to eat.

Oh, look at that!
Do you see that?
Can you do that?
Yes, you can.
You can do it, too.

One, two, three.
GO!
No, that is not good.
That is too little.

Now, here we go.
One, two, three.
Oh, my! Oh, my!
Look at that!
That is good!

Here you are with me.
And here I am with you.
Oh, what a happy day, dear dragon.

The following activities support the findings of the National Reading Panel that determined the most effective components for reading instruction are: Phonemic Awareness, Phonics, Vocabulary, Fluency, and Text Comprehension.

Phonemic Awareness: The /g/ sound

Oral Blending: Say the beginning and ending sounds of the following words and ask your child to listen to the sounds and say the whole word:

ba + /g/ = bag	di + /g/ = dig	sa + /g/ = sag
bi + /g/ = big	le + /g/ = leg	ta + /g/ = tag
pe + /g/ = peg	dra + /g/ = drag	fla + /g/ = flag
pi + /g/ = pig		

Phonics: The letter Gg

1. Demonstrate how to form the letters **G** and **g** for your child.

2. Have your child practice writing **G** and **g** at least three times each.

3. Ask your child to point to the words in the book that start with the letter **g**.

4. Write down the following words and ask your child to circle the letter **g** in each word:

go	glad	tag	get	flag	guess
tiger	give	target	gave	dig	got
rag	gum	finger	good		

Vocabulary: Homophones

1. Find the words *to, too,* and *two* in the book. Read the sentences that include each word.

2. Explain to your child that words that sound the same but have different meanings are called homophones.

3. Write each word on a piece of paper. Say sentences including each word and ask your child to point to the correct word for each sentence. For example, which one goes with "I am going (to) the store." Or "There are (two) shoes in a pair."

Fluency: Choral Reading

1. Reread the story with your child at least two more times while your child tracks the print by running a finger under the words as they are read. Ask your child to read the words he or she knows with you.

2. Reread the story aloud together. Be careful to read at a rate that your child can keep up with.

3. Repeat choral reading and allow your child to be the lead reader and ask him or her to change from a whisper to a loud voice while you follow along and change your voice.

Text Comprehension: Discussion Time

1. Ask your child to retell the sequence of events in the story.

2. To check comprehension, ask your child the following questions:

   • What is the object that the boy and Dear Dragon made go up the pole?

   • What holiday do you think the family is celebrating? What happened in the story to make you think that?

   • How did Dear Dragon help the family on page 23?

   • What is your favorite holiday? Why?

WORD LIST

Let's Go, Dear Dragon uses the 65 words listed below.

This list can be used to practice reading the words that appear in the text. You may wish to write the words on index cards and use them to help your child build automatic word recognition. Regular practice with these words will enhance your child's fluency in reading connected text.

a	eat	I	one	up
am		in	out	us
and	father	is		
are	for	it	play	want
at	fun			we
away		like	ride	what
	get	little		where
big	go	look	see	will
	good		something	with
can	guess	make		work(s)
car		me	that	
come	happy	mother	the	yes
	have	my	this	you
day	help		three	
dear	here	no	to	
do		not	too	
dragon		now	two	
		oh		

ABOUT THE AUTHOR Margaret Hillert has written over 80 books for children who are just learning to read. Her books have been translated into many different languages and over a million children throughout the world have read her books. She first started writing poetry as a child and has continued to write for children and adults throughout her life. A first grade teacher for 34 years, Margaret is now retired from teaching and lives in Michigan where she likes to write, take walks in the morning, and care for her three cats.

Photograph by Glenna Washburn

ABOUT THE ADVISER Shannon Cannon contributed the activities pages that appear in this book. Shannon serves as a literacy consultant and provides staff development to help improve reading instruction. She is a frequent presenter at educational conferences and workshops. Prior to this she worked as an elementary school teacher and as president of a curriculum publishing company.